Salam

Amelie Kaas

DEDICATION

To my grandfather Dr.W.Pieter Kaas who died Febuary 2016.

Amelie Kaas

ACKNOWLEDGMENTS

Thanks to my mum Rachel Kaas for
helping and supporting me throughout
the stories development.
Thanks to my best friend Johanna Rind
for inspiring me and giving me advice
for my story.
Most of all thanks to my lovely chair for
being really comfortable.

CHAPTER 1
FATHER'S DEATH

Bang! Boom!

The gunshots were droning in my ears. I ran faster and faster, the buildings crumbling down behind us. Others stumbled across the ruins so that they could escape. Arran ran on ahead quickly and carefully. He ducked under beams, climbing over the ruins that were once our homes. My heart was beating quicker and quicker, thumping so loud I was sure that others could hear it too.

Rashid ran next to mother, grabbing her hand and clinging onto it. The dusty ground felt hard uhknder my bare feet and the dry air was stinging in my throat. Arran ran further and further away from us, sprinting on ahead. We were not the only ones. Left, right, ahead and behind - everywhere people were fleeing. Each and everyone had planned a risky escape to finally be able to live in peace.

I have grown up knowing nothing else but war, death and sorrow, I cannot remember how life was before the war started four years ago. After father's death everything changed. Mother warned us before he died. She said our thoughts, opinions and ideas have to stay private. Father never wanted Syria to be like this. He wanted freedom. He wanted to be able to decide things, vote for things, even be able to change things if it was best for us.

After father's death mother said, "Bashar al-Assad thinks he owns us. He thinks he can do and say what he wants. But father never, never would let him do it. He protested for it day and night, just to have more rights and freedom." One evening as the sun was setting, father was protesting alongside thousands of other people. Bashar al-Assad's army was there, standing between the protestants and the old broken mosque. Bashar al-Assad does not want other people to choose and decide things for the country.

He killed father, and with him thousands of Syrians that wanted more rights. The rest of my family, including me, had already planned to flee. First we are traveling towards Lebanon. After that we will use a boat to cross the ocean and arrive in Italy. After we arrive there we are traveling on until we reach Austria. As soon as we reach Germany we will be safe.

Our home was destroyed by Bashar al-Assad's army two days ago, and ISIS is not making it any easier. Arran and mother miss father most. Arran used to play outside and go fishing with father, during a time called peace.

CHAPTER 2
PEACE

The word peace rolls over your tongue almost as nicely as the actual meaning. Peace. I have tried to picture peace over and over again, but it is almost impossible to imagine something you only know the opposite of. If there would be peace in Syria I could go to school again and learn things like I used to. Our school was bombed one year ago, and since then I've been browsing through Arran's old school books to continue learning.

My favorite subject used to be maths or art. I'm not sure why I liked maths. It just came easily to me. Art was simply the most creative subject. It gave me a chance to forget my thoughts of Bashar al-Assad and war. When we arrive in Germany my biggest wish is to be able to go to school again and be inspired by numbers and enjoy being artistic.

A lot of other Syrians had told us how their families had already made it to Germany and were now living in peace. Others said their families died or starved as they fled. Mother acted as if she never believed them, but all of us knew it was true. The trips were dangerous, followed by nightmares and injuries that stayed with you for the rest of your   life.

Mother has a weak left leg. She had an operation and years later when all the medicine was kept for Syrian soldiers her leg got infected. It began to swell and yellow pus covered the wound. Her injury is still an open sore and doctors say it will never heal. People think it is impossible that the injury will not heal but all of the skin around the wound has died and has turned yellow and wrinkled.

When mother had the idea to flee, everyone thought she was crazy. They thought she was too weak and said she would need a walking stick. Since the war started, we do not have much money and mother looks very weak and skinny. Before father's death, mother, Arran and father had plenty to eat and enough medicine for mother.

For some time we have not been earning enough money. Mother is trying to bring in some money by washing or cooking for people, but it is no good. She never earns enough to feed all of us two proper meals a day. She risks her life for ours, by feeding us before herself. Arran has looked for work but people insist he is too young, although he is already thirteen.

CHAPTER 3
BEFORE WAR ERUPTED

Arran is the type of brother you can always rely on. Before war hit our village we were allowed to play outside like every other Syrian child. Arran and I used to play with sticks and stones, and if father was in a good mood, he let us play with a special ball. The ball was a shade of dark brown leather and father would oil the leather ball with a thick layer of grease. Father never told us why he greased the ball, and we never asked.

As war came closer we were not allowed to go outside anymore. It was too dangerous. My friend Nour used to love to play on the streets with me but after what happened to her mother, she and her father fled to Jordan. One evening Nour's mother never returned from shopping. No-one ever heard of her again. Everyone in the village knew she died, but each time a villager saw Nour or her father, they tried to smile at them.

Nour and I used to cry and share our stories together. We hugged and talked with each other whenever we could, but it usually ended in tears. Before war turned our village upside down we had toy shops, grocery stores and lots more. Shops closed or got bombed and now there are only health organizations that provide clothes and food.

Health organizations also distributed medicine, water, school materials and books. Arran would run to the main square to collect the supplies we would need, such as clothes, food and water. Before war hit Syria I had bright clothes: dresses, blouses and lots of expensive outfits. When one day Arran came home with a pretty red dress I could not understand why organizations were handing out such nice clothes.

The dress was bright red and had a pretty felt flower sewn onto the front. The material felt soft and mother called it silk. I didn't wear the dress a lot and it was much too big anyway. I wear large shirts handed down by Arran. I also wear loose, baggy trousers made of cotton that have been handed down by Arran. I like loose clothing. It is comfortable and easy to wear on hot days.

Arran works hard to get food and water from the organizations that provide them, but if you are late, all the food, water and clothes have already been handed out. That is why mother and Arran work to earn money. With the money we can go to the market which is the only place which still sells things.

Fleeing is difficult. Running and walking was exhausting on the first day. Rashid worried most. He knew all about the dangers that lay ahead of us. All of us worry, even I do. I have never been anywhere other than Syria and I am not sure if Rashid even knows that there is a different world out there. Rashid never went to school - he was too young - and he won't until we reach Germany.

Before we fled there was not enough time to pack what was necessary. We just threw what we had into backpacks and left. Like others, war forced us to move on and away. We had to disappear.

CHAPTER 4
FLEEING

The dusty ground helped reduce the sharpness of each stone and protected our feet. It was a hot sunny day when we left. I was wearing Arran's old grey trousers and a light blue shirt which looked nice and clean because mother and I had washed a few clothes in our water tub.

The water tub was a container that stood in front of our house and would collect rain water. We used the water to bath and wash, sometimes even drank it. Mother did not like to drink from it. She said anything could have evaporated into the clouds, even disgusting things that we don't want to drink.

In my backpack I had packed two more shirts and two extra pairs of trousers. Also I had packed the red dress so that I could wear it when we reached Italy or Germany. I took an old plastic water bottle too. The good thing about it is that I can refill it. I also stuffed a pair of sandals in my bag so I can wear them later on. Arran found them in the market and bought them for me because they match my red dress.

Mother does not want me wearing the shoes because she says that the sandals will wear out.

Mother had a few coins and a lot of food and water. She had sewn two larger notes in the bottom of each rucksack, knowing that we would have to pay to cross the ocean. She had shown this to us but made us promise not to touch the money until we were at the coast. Our bags were heavy and the continual movement made it feel even heavier. We didn't know when we would arrive in Lebanon but we knew we had to keep going. Mother wanted to reach Lebanon's border in the next few weeks. She said we would walk day and night, but we knew the days would be dangerous. We tried to keep to main roads but often had to take an alternative route when convoys of Syrian soldiers rolled by.

We come from a village close to Masyaf which is not too far from Lebanon's border. Our village was almost completely burned down and all of us know we are not going to come back to Syria ever again. If the war stops, we will not have enough money to return, unless mother finds a good job in Germany and can finance our ticket home.

Mother wants to protect us and do what is best for everyone. But she knows, as well as I do, that not all of us will make it to Germany. It will be very dangerous, especially if we start running low on important supplies. When we get onto the boat. the chances that we will starve are high enough to worry about it, day and night.

CHAPTER 5
LEBANON'S BORDER

The sun was shining lazily on the dusty ground. It felt as hot as if you were touching the sun's surface with your bare hands.. We had been walking alone day after day, legs aching so badly that none of us could move properly. Our food supplies were running low, and we had not been able to refill our water bottles for some hours. There had been no other Syrian refugees in sight and this was a surprise to us. Where were all the others who were fleeing?

That afternoon we finally caught up with a group of twelve other Syrians. They gave us some milk that they had stolen from a stray goat. We were glad of its refreshment and drank it greedily. We continued for some time when suddenly a fence came into view. Some cheered while others sighed, but everyone was afraid about crossing the border. When there was only half a kilometer between us and the border, we could see the soldiers guarding the fenced boundary.

"Move back!" shouted a soldier in a dark creamy

uniform. He was tall with grey, tousled hair. His uniform had two medals pinned to the breast pocket.

"We need to get onto a boat!" cried one of the other refugees. He was definitely suffering and his arms were really skinny and so were his legs. " Well we won't let you pass!" said a second soldier scornfully who had become interested in our group and marched over towards us. The second soldier was a chubby man and had curly brown hair that ran down the back of his neck.

" We need to get across, please!" said another Syrian, who really needed help. His two sons were supporting him on either side. His arms were dangling across the boy's shoulders, his weak legs were scratched and bloody.

" We can't take any more of you!" shouted the chubby man, pointing his gun at one of the man's boys.

" Please, we need your help!" mother said weakly, suffering in silence.

" Well, well, well, madam. Tell you what. You won't cross here. Go somewhere else!" mocked the chubby man, grinning from ear to ear. He had slid his gun back into his belt and walked towards a grey tall tent.

" No passing here!" he shouted over his shoulder.

The taller man marched into the same tent and left us standing in front of the five meter high fence. The fence was electric and scared us all.

" There is only one way into Lebanon!" said one of the boys, pointing. Everyone turned to look where he was

11

pointing. Both boys had scruffy brown hair. They looked like twins although they were not identical. There, between two poles was a hole in the bottom of the fence.

The fence was buzzing and zipping loudly. Many of us were scared that the soldiers would come back, but soon a lovely smell of soup reached our nostrils.

" They are having lunch!" Arran said. I was not sure if he wanted to reassure us, or if he wanted to warn us. Suddenly all of us surged towards the hole, staring at it, wondering how we would squeeze into Lebanon.

CHAPTER 6
SQUEEZING INTO LEBANON

The fence was rusty, and as we came closer to the metal barrier, we kept an eye on the entrance of the tent. Everyone gathered quietly around the hole, glaring at it as if they could make the hole bigger just by staring at it. One of the boys started digging with his bare hands at the bottom of the slashed wire, making the gap bigger. The size of it made it possible for everyone to pass into Lebanon.

The boy who had dug the hole was the first to slide underneath it and waited impatiently for the next person on the other side. He smiled over to his brother and father who were sitting, resting and eating a shriveled fruit for energy. A man who was standing behind me pushed me forward. The hole was easily big enough for me to crawl underneath the fence. Next a woman with blonde long hair slid through, her long hair dragging across the ground. As soon as the woman was through, she ran over a hill and disappeared.

Rashid crawled underneath the fence, just as I had. It was embarrassing that I was three years older and he was only a bit shorter. Next Arran slid through the gap and, all of a sudden, he stood next to me calling mother across.

" Mother, come on!" Arran cried, staring at the tent. Next mother started sliding through. All of a sudden her shoe got caught and she stumbled. She was stiff from the walk and her injured leg was bothering her.

The tent's entrance opened and the two soldiers burst out. Arran was pulling on mother's shoe trying to loosen it. The chubby soldier pulled out his gun and started shooting in the direction of mother and Arran.

" Arran, come quickly!" I screamed behind me, as the older boy grabbed my hand and started to run. Suddenly the shots were coming faster and louder!

Arran dropped to his death, blood pouring out of his throat. Mother bent down to help him, but the shots reached her. The bullets were too accurate and mother dropped too. As I ran with my head turned back, all I could see was a spreading pool of blood surrounding my family. I blocked the image from my mind and ran with silent tears streaming down my cheeks. I made no sound but simply stumbled on, as my instinct to survive took over.

The boy ran further and further, urging me on. I simply followed. After an eternity we reached the safety of a village. Only now did I see that he had been carrying Rashid all the way.

CHAPTER 7
I AM TAREK

The boy sat Rashid on the ground next to me and swung his backpack off his back. He zipped open his bag and pulled out a brown box. He took off the lid and inside was something that looked like a chunk of silver. He handed one of the chunks to me and took another out of the box. I stared at him, not knowing what to do. He started pulling a layer of silver off the chunk.

" It's just foil!" he said staring at me as if he had read my mind.

I tried to tear away the foil from my chunk and it came off easily. " Is it a sandwich?" I asked, looking down at my slice of bread.

" Yeah, it is bread, chicken and tomato. We were lucky to find a kind farmer who made us these after my brother and I helped him in the fields for a day!" he answered, as if it was obvious. I took a bite and to be honest, it was the best thing I had eaten in years. He ripped his sandwich in half and handed one half to Rashid.

Rashid greedily grabbed his half out of the boy's hand. The boy wiped Rashid's last tears from his cheeks and ruffled Rashid's hair. Rashid ate quicker than I did, and was done in a few seconds. The boy ate his sandwich carefully and kept staring at the path we had come, in case one of the soldiers appeared.

" I am Tarek!" said the boy after he finished his food.

" That is Rashid and I am Liliane!" I said, pointing at Rashid. Rashid yawned loudly as he lay back.

" I think we should rest." Tarek said standing up slowly. He took us to an empty doorway and made us hide in the corner of a deserted building where we slept for several hours. We shared our sad stories and he told us of the mother he too had lost and the life he had left. We stayed there for a couple of days, hoping one of our relatives would stumble through the village but no-one came.

After a time we decided to move on, traveling together. The days turned into weeks. We journeyed on towards the coast, three children alone. No-one bothered us. It was as if we were invisible. We fed from the fields, finding buried potatoes that were forgotten in the harvest and sometimes berries and wild fruits. Tarek left us hidden in a field a couple of times and worked on Lebanese farms to earn cheese and cold meats or a container of cold milk.

We were getting thinner and thinner and weaker and weaker but knew we had to keep moving. Some weeks later we entered a village and saw seagulls overhead and knew we were finally at the coast. We found a quiet spot in the shade of an olive tree and settled ourselves down.

Rashid was exhausted and glad of the rest. He took out his blanket from his backpack and made himself a comfortable corner to sleep.

"Stay here while I go and search for the harbor." Tarek said, standing up slowly. I knew it was time to risk our luck and try and find a way to cross the sea. The image of my mother sewing the notes into the bottom of my rucksack flashed in my mind.

"OK. But wait! I have something hidden in the bottom of my backpack" I cried as I emptied the contents onto the ground. I asked Tarek for his knife and carefully cut around the package my mother had planted there many months ago. The notes were damp and faded but still intact and I handed them to Tarek.

"Take these and see if you can find someone who will take us with them on their boat." I murmured, a tear falling down my cheek as I spoke. Tarek hugged me, grabbed a few coins from his bag and ran off into the shadows that fell from the low buildings.

Rashid opened one eye and asked in a whisper, " Will he come back soon?" I stared at Rashid before I answered. " I don't know, let's hope he does!"

Rashid closed his eyes and started breathing heavily. I pulled my backpack of my back and lay down next to Rashid. I could not fall asleep, I kept thinking about Mother and Arran. Questions started buzzing through my mind making me worry even more. But at some point I must have drifted into a deep sleep

When I woke up, Tarek was sitting next to me. " You slept the whole afternoon and all through the night!" Tarek said not taking his eyes off of sleeping Rashid.

" Did you find the harbor?" I asked him, rubbing my tired eyes.

" Yeah I did. I even managed to get us some tickets for a boat trip across the ocean. We will make it to Italy!" he answered excitedly. Rashid opened his eyes to the sound of this and asked just what I had asked. Tarek repeated his answer, but this time added the boat's name, LUCY.

We packed up and threw our bags over our backs. Then we quickly hurried down the alley ways, always walking further and further, deeper and deeper into the village, Tarek holding my and Rashid's hands, as he led the way to the harbor.

CHAPTER 8
LUCY

The town was small and there were a lot of people lying on the street. We had no idea where we were in Lebanon. All we knew was that we were getting closer and closer to the ocean. The sound of the waves hitting against the rocks lay ahead of us. We had been walking for hours - our only target was the harbour. Lebanon's heat was impossible to cope with. The sun's beams were stretching themselves down intensely into the villages streets.

Suddenly there was a big open space, with benches, statues, a fountain and trees filling up the unused areas. Rashid was about to step into the open from our alleyway when Tarek roughly pulled him back.

" We need to walk around the square!" whispered Tarek, his voice filled with alarm."

Why do we have to take the long way?" asked Rashid loudly. Tarek stared at Rashid, his eyes saying something like, "don't speak that loudly".

All of a sudden a soldier walked past the alleyway we were in. Tarek slapped us against a house wall, holding his index finger to his lips. Once the soldier had walked by, we ran back a few metres and then turned right.

"Why is the chubby man here?" asked Rashid completely shocked.

" He might be looking for us!" Tarek answered, worrying. Rashid ran off, forcing us to follow.

He ran straight ahead and turned sharply right. We ran after him and suddenly the harbour shimmered in front of us. Rashid stopped and stared in amazement. From here on Tarek took the lead. He led us towards a little, wooden boat which had a name painted on the side: "LUCY". The boat looked like it could only carry fifteen or so people, but it was obvious that they would overload.

We walked towards an old, gnarled olive tree which offered shade and set up our camp at the trees thick roots. Tarek handed me his last few coins and said I had to get all the food I could for the trip. He laid out an old blanket and a heavy jumper, making a bed for Rashid. He shooed me away. I walked across the pavement and entered a small, dark shop. I bought twelve loaves of bread, a bundle of unripe bananas, three bottles of water and more. My arms ached under the weight of our supplies. As I left the store there was a tune playing further down the road. I walked towards the sound, and there, on the edge of the pavement, sat a man.

The man was playing an instrument that looked like a huge pear. I recognised the tune. Father used to play it on his violin. Each night before going to bed he would play for us. He said it was a tune his own father used to play for him.

After father died, the violin was no use to us because none of us could play it. Mother sold it for a fair price so that we could buy food, water and new clothes.

The man stopped playing as I approached and smiled up at me. I smiled back.

"Where did you learn how to play that song?" I asked him. I knew I was not allowed to speak to strangers but this was another Syrian refugee.

"My mother taught me!" he answered, smiling broadly.

"I am Liliane!" I said staring at his instrument.

"I am Jonathan, but all my friends call me Guitar Joe!" said the man whose smile seemed to be frozen on his face.

" Am I a friend?" I asked, looking at him intently.

"Now you are!" He said firmly, as I left to return to the olive tree.

CHAPTER 9
GUITAR JOE

I ran all the way back to where Tarek and Rashid lay asleep. I dropped my shopping bag and sat down next to the boys. My throat was sore and my eyes were dry. The air was hot and dusty and my whole body ached from top to bottom. It was late in the afternoon when the boys finally awoke and the light was fading. They sat up carefully and watched me unpack what I had bought. In the bag there were only twelve loaves of bread.

"Is that all you bought?" asked Tarek shocked.

"No!...I must have left the other bag at Guitar Joe's camp!" I shouted loudly, straight into Tarek's face.

"Who is Guitar Joe?" Rashid asked, staring at me.

"Guitar Joe is my friend!" I said quickly before I ran off. Tarek ran after me and Rashid followed Tarek who was chasing me wildly. I ran past the shop and dashed further and further towards the guitar's flowing melody.

Guitar Joe sat on the pavement playing his guitar. I stopped in front of him, completely out of breath.

"Hello Liliane!" Guitar Joe greeted me.

"Do you know if I left a shopping bag here?" I asked Guitar Joe in panic as Tarek suddenly appeared behind me.

" Oh yes! Yes, of course!" answered Guitar Joe cheerfully. He handed me my bag and looked at Tarek and me curiously.

"Are you children travelling alone?" he enquired, as Rashid suddenly appeared from nowhere.

"Well, we have got one another!" Tarek answered, trying to stop the tears from flowing. He was thinking of his family.

" Well I'm getting onto a boat called Lucy tomorrow!" Guitar Joe started, before Rashid interrupted.

"Our boat is also called Lucy and is leaving tomorrow!" Rashid shouted excitedly.

" Well... If you want to we could travel together. It will give us a better chance to get on the boat and then into France!" Guitar Joe said, almost as excitedly as Rashid.

" Well I guess if it is that helpful it can't harm us!" agreed Tarek.

"Help me pack up and I'll join you!" Guitar Joe cried, stuffing blankets and other objects into his bags. Guitar Joe placed his guitar in my hands. Suddenly I felt important. I was carrying a really special musical instrument. Guitar Joe followed us, carrying two bags in each hand. He was a average sized man. His blue eyes seemed to calm me, and so did his thick curly red hair. He had a few freckles here and there, but otherwise he looked just like every other man in his twenties.

Guitar Joe walked proudly. His upper body was straight, and his head held high. Tarek and Rashid dragged their legs after them, stumbling towards our camp. I watched Guitar Joe carefully and tried to copy him whenever I could. I was tired. My legs walked and my body followed.

When we reached our camp I placed my bag next to the other and lay down. Guitar Joe had a lot of bags, all of them were stuffed with food. I wanted to stay awake but my eyes closed and I could not help but fall asleep. I woke up a few times and listened to Guitar Joe playing his guitar softly but I never opened my eyes. I did not have the strength to watch Guitar Joe make his hands flow over the guitar's strings. The melody lulled me into a deeper and deeper sleep.

CHAPTER 10
OVERLOAD

When I awoke a sun's beam was tickling my nose. The sun was dawning and Guitar Joe's melody was singing across the streets. Guitar Joe's bags were stacked and ready to leave. My bag was already packed, and was ready to grab and jump onto the boat. Rashid was chewing on a loaf of bread and Tarek was still asleep. His quiet breathing and closed eyes were lighted up by another beam that shone down from the sun.

I ripped a piece off Rashid's loaf and stuffed it into my mouth. Bread was one of the only things I had eaten in the last few days. My stomach grumbled and my lungs were screaming for water. We could not waste the water though, we needed it for the trip.

Guitar Joe stood up and walked towards sleeping Tarek.

" Tarek, wake up!" he whispered as he shook Tarek by the shoulders. Tarek opened one eye and then the other.

" Come on, the boat is about to leave!" Guitar Joe added, pulling Tarek to his feet. Tarek stood up and walked towards his bags.

" Are we going now?" asked Tarek stuffing his clothes into bag.

" Well when else are we going to go?!" Guitar Joe answered.

Rashid grabbed his backpack and stood there shifting his weight from one side to the other.

" Rashid, stop stressing us and help take the bags!" I shouted demandingly.

" Oh, he's fine!" Guitar Joe said, grabbing a bag in each hand. I swung my backpack onto my back and snatched our two shopping bags. Guitar Joe strapped his guitar onto Tarek's back, who was carrying his own bag and Guitar Joe's last bag.

"Are we ready?" asked Guitar Joe as we started approaching the first few boats.

" Yes!" Tarek, Rashid and I answered excitedly. When Lucy stood in front of us we were shocked. There were too many other refugees on the boat. I worried whether the boat would sink.

" Tickets please!" shouted a man with a funny accent. Tarek handed Guitar Joe our tickets, so that it looked like we were a group.

" Here you go!" Guitar Joe said passing the papers to the man.

" You can find a free spot to rest!" the man said. Guitar Joe led the way onto the boat. Rashid held my hand, his worries surfacing. I wanted to comfort him, but I was struggling with my own fears. Would the boat sink? There was no time to worry, we were all scared. Guitar Joe fought his way through the over-crowded boat, making sure we were behind him.

"Here there is enough space!" Guitar Joe finally announced. I threw the bags onto the small, clear space on deck and placed my backpack next to Rashid's backpack.

" Are we going to be on this boat for long?" Rashid asked.

No one answered him, probably because everyone was too busy thinking of the most realistically dreadful way to die. I was sure I would drown or starve, but I did not want to scare Rashid any more.

CHAPTER 11
SEA SICKNESS

Lucy was a long, thin wooden boat. It had a chestnut brown hull which was polished. The boat was far too big and heavy for the small motor at the back. The waves washed against the boat's side, swaying it from left to right. The boat smelt of fish and vomit. I leaned onto the boat's rim and peered over the edge. There was a shoal of fish swimming underneath and a flock of seagulls were soaring above my head, screeching loudly.

There were about fifty Syrians squeezed together on the Lucy. Lucy was already about to sink as we left the harbour. The boat sat so low in the water that my fingers could stroke across the surface of the waves. A skinny old man sat at the boat's motor, looking out to sea. On our right sat a young Syrian couple who were clinging onto each other as if their life depended on it. On our left, sat a lonely bony woman with a baby resting on her lap. The people on the boat were thin and hungry. Most of us were too worried to unpack warmer clothes or food as any movement made the boat rock dangerously.

As the boat started to leave the harbour, a lot of people turned white in their faces or started to cry. Tears also ran down my cheeks, leaving a salty taste in my mouth. Rashid was trying to stabilize himself, but did not succeed. He was flung from left to right and bashed into other Syrians, I felt like everyone was smiling at him. The boat cut its way through the waves and soared along the ocean's surface.

Guitar Joe unpacked his guitar and played tune after tune. I watched Lebanon's coast get further and further away. The boat shook about, wobbling us from left to right. I felt sick inside so I lay down next to Guitar Joe. Guitar Joe played on and on, keeping everyone entertained. There were about ten children including us on the boat.

A few people turned green and pale because of the rocking waves. Suddenly something was sliding up my throat. I ran to the rail just before the vomit came pouring out. Tarek hurried towards me and made sure I was alright. I was not the only one feeling sick, all around us people were vomiting the little food they had eaten.

I remember collapsing, but nothing more. All of a sudden everything went dark. I was frightened inside and outside I had fainted.

I pictured mother, Arran, Rashid and me playing hide and seek in our house like we used to. I wished times could stay like they were, or go back in time. I'm not sure if mother and Arran are alive, but I know if they are, we will not see them again. It is like a playback, seeing mother and Arran getting shot time and time again. When I wake up I will ask Tarek if they are alive. My mind is spinning from picture to memory and back.

Memories flooded my thoughts. Everything went blurry and darkness appeared again. In front of me blackness covered pictures of memories and hopes. I wanted to push the black out of my way, but I could not. I wanted to wake up but I didn't. I wanted to stand up and shout " I'm alive!" But my body lay still and silent. I had enough time to rest my body, but I don't know for how long I did.

CHAPTER 12
STORM

After a few times of falling asleep and waking up from my coma I woke up for real from " the dead". I felt something soft stroking my cheek, and when I tried to open my eyes, they flickered and then finally opened. Sunlight flowed into sight. Tarek smiled at me as he took his hand off my cheek. People gathered all around me. Rashid sat next to me leaning back onto Guitar Joe's chest.

"You're alright!" Rashid announced clapping his hands. I smiled at him, but when I saw the thunder clouds, my smile left.

"The storm will be here in an hour or two!" Guitar Joe said, looking up.

"There's no way around them!" cried our neighbor with the baby on her lap. The woman had a funny accent, and the baby just made weird noises such as " Grunt"

Guitar Joe handed me a loaf of bread which I could not

wait to eat.

"How long was I asleep?" I asked staring at Tarek.

"About a week or so!" Tarek answered. I chewed the loaf as the storm came closer and closer. The thunder roared louder and louder, deafening my ears. The clouds scared me as the blackness shadowed the whole ocean around us.

"Can you swim?" Guitar Joe asked us, as two lightning bolts struck through the sky.

"No, I can't!" I screamed at the top of my lungs.

The waves shook the boat about, the sky produced a scary atmosphere. My heart pounded as the wind grew stronger and stronger. All of a sudden a chubby man was flung over the boat's side.

"Help! I can't swim!" he shouted, clinging to the side. Guitar Joe ran over to help lift the man out of the water but the man's grip slipped as he let go.

Rashid ran to the railing to watch, but the man never came up again. That had only been the beginning. People were flung overboard and as they tried to save others. The woman next to us was sucked off her blanket and smashed against a wave. I watched with alarm as suddenly I felt my body being lifted up by the wind. I clung onto the rail and when the wind gave up I crashed back onto the boat.

I leapt to my feet and ran towards where Tarek had been standing. He had been drawn into the ocean and came up again and again. I was there to watch him take his last breath. He sank down to the ocean's floor.

"Nooo!" I shouted, as his red shirt was not able to be seen any more. People were flying everywhere, and when finally the wind calmed down, everyone ran to check if their food and clothes was still there.

About twenty five people died that day, which was half of the people onboard at the beginning. When I went around looking for Guitar Joe and Rashid, I found neither. I peered across the ocean, and there floating withinin reach was Rashid's dead body. An old woman walked towards me and handed me Guitar Joe's guitar case.

"I'm sorry, he drowned!" she said, pointing to the horizon. I was alone.

CHAPTER 13
REMAINS

Days passed and no one talked to me. I ate and drank until the last of my food was gone. My neighbours were all silent, well most of them. The baby that had been sleeping in a secured basket, kept on blabbering on and on as if it was talking to someone that was not even there. I had not paid a lot of attention to the baby until now. It had bright blue eyes and short, curly blond hair, similar to an angel. No one would starve, I thought, but all around people were suffering.

I knew I should not, but I emptied Guitar Joe's food into my own bag and acted like I had enough to last for ever. I remembered how days ago our boat had been swimming in dead bodies and vomit. Memories were the strongest when night time drew near. I could picture Rashid's dead body floating on the ocean's surface, his face pale and his eyes completely white.

I am only ten, not old enough to fend for myself. I won't survive.

I have been on the boat for ages. People started fishing, hunting fish to eat. We had built a fire in the middle of the boat which was made of driftwood and seaweed. A wet plastic bag prevented the fire from burning down the whole boat. Everyone shared and when I tried seaweed I wanted to spit it out again, but I forced it down my throat. The terrible taste was dripping down my throat, the chewy weed clinging to my teeth.

One day it was like a candle had been lit in the darkness of my misery. My neighbour had been starving herself, trying to keep her baby alive, and she had not moved since last week only to feed the baby. Now she turned to me, her eyes reflecting her pain. With one hand she was stroking her baby's hair, with the other she was fumbling in her pocket. The baby was chewing on its shirt as the mother   kissed   its   head.

With her final strength, she spluttered out her last words. " Please take my dear baby Florence. I can't take the pain any longer!" She pulled money out of her pocket.

"Take this and please make sure Florence survives!" she said shoving Florence in my direction. The baby smiled at me, showing her small milk teeth pushing through her gum. I froze., I only noticed that I had picked the baby out of her mother's hands as the baby lay on my lap.

"Wait, why me?" I asked as the mother shut her eyes.

"Thank you!" she said, before her breathing stopped.

"Why me?" I asked again and again in my mind. The woman had not answered.

Two tall men walked over to me. " Is the woman

dead?" one of the men asked as he stared at Florence's mother. I nodded slowly as the baby curled its small hands around my finger. I watched the men march away before I examined Florence's face.

She looked as if she was from a catalogue. Her face was so pretty, as if everything had been measured to fit. When the men came back and searched her mother's pockets I knew what would happen. Before they picked her up I wanted to reach out and stop them, to keep her with us, but I did not have the strength. The tip of my finger caught on something metal and pulled off Florence's mothers necklace. The men hurried away, and before I could stop them, they had thrown the mother's body overboard.

CHAPTER 14
FLORENCE

The necklace rested on the palm of my hand. Hanging from it was a small pendant. The pendant was as gold as the chain and had a small angel engraved on it. At first I thought it was Florence, but then I saw the angel's wings, and realised it could not be her. I didn't want to have something so special to look after, so I attached it to Florence's neck.

She turned her head and smiled broadly at me. I felt Florence's smile warm me to the bone. I fed her some mashed carrot and then I held her in both hands. I knew I was not to keep her, not alone, but I rested her calmly on my hip as I walked along the slippery deck. It was difficult to balance, and when I finally reached the first woman, I stopped and, only with a lot of effort, I managed to stay standing.

"Would you like her?" I asked quietly.

"No!" Said the woman and shooed me away.

Quickly I hurried along the deck, asking everyone I passed. No luck, I was not able to get rid of Florence. Maybe Florence's mother gave her to me for a good reason. I kept thinking about it, over and over, but it was hard to believe. I am normal, or not? I drifted off to sleep with her snuggled beside me.

When I finally woke up Florence was nowhere to be seen. I jumped to my feet and felt my stiff legs ache as I dashed across the boat.

"Florence!" I exclaimed as I saw her resting in an older woman's lap.

"Is she yours?" she asked in a rough Syrian voice.

"Yes!" I answered as the woman pressed Florence into my arms.

"Take good care of her, won't you ?!" said the woman smiling at Florence.

As I turned away I saw Florence reach out and wave to the woman. Her small fingers were stretched out, her wrist shaking loosely. The woman waved back, and blew kisses straight at Florence. Florence enjoyed being tickled under her chest and at the base of her feet. As we reached our mat I let Florence jiggle about, giggling her head off as I tickled her.

Florence and I got to know each other as the days passed by. I did take care of her, more than I did of myself.

CHAPTER 15
BELIEVE

There is no way of keeping track of time out at sea. How long have I been here? When will I see land again? Questions buzzing around in my head make it hard to concentrate. I can't eat anything. Whatever I eat comes back out the same way it came in. I know I have no chance of making it to Italy. I will starve. I have been too busy keeping Florence alive, to the point that I have had no time to eat myself. I know if I don`t eat, I will turn crazy. Eating is important. It's where you get your energy from. If I don`t eat my body will start using my body`s fat to get energy. I feel dizzy stroking Florence`s soft silky hair. It`s as if I can feel my body eating its own fat to survive. I cannot sit up any more. My body aches at the slightest thought of movement. The sun sets and rises. As each new day awakens, more and more pain rushes down my body. My eyes open and close as hallucination starts. No water has led to dehydration. It hurts to breathe. My breath is heavy. I know I won`t last long.

I knew the moment I opened my eyes, that this was the

last time. Florence`s head rested on my shoulder as I watched her eat a chunk of stale bread. Her blue eyes looked at me carefully as I spluttered out my last words.

"Florence, get to Italy...and never go back home!" I muttered, trying to speak clearly. "I believe in you...and I know by the time you get to Germany you will be safe!"

I cannot get the last few words out. I feel my body shutting down as I try to say one last thing.

" Believe!" Just as my eyes shut I spit out the last sounds.

Everything turned black, as finally, I experienced peace.

Through the silent darkness, a well-known hand reached for me. I felt my fingertips stroke the open palm of his hand, as I reached out to grab it. I was pulled out of the blackness and flung myself across my father's neck. I breathed in the smell of my father, the scent of his pipe smoke and I rubbed my cheek against his prickly beard.

"Salam Lili!" said his familiar voice, as I let go of life.

ABOUT THE AUTHOR

I'm Amelie Kaas an eleven year old from ZIS. I'm in the MUN team 2016 which is where I got the idea to write about Refugees from. I found out about the Syrian Refugee crisis on the news. This is my finished story.

15644077R00030

Printed in Great Britain
by Amazon